SCORNED FURY

BY

JASON HARRY

Order this book online at www.trafford.com/07-2631
or email orders@trafford.com

Most Trafford titles are also available at major online book retailers.

© Copyright 2008 Jason Harry.

All rights reserved. No part of this publication may be reproduced, stored in a retrieval system, or transmitted, in any form or by any means, electronic, mechanical, photocopying, recording, or otherwise, without the written prior permission of the author.

Note for Librarians: A cataloguing record for this book is available from Library and Archives Canada at www.collectionscanada.ca/amicus/index-e.html

ISBN: 978-1-4251-5833-0

We at Trafford believe that it is the responsibility of us all, as both individuals and corporations, to make choices that are environmentally and socially sound. You, in turn, are supporting this responsible conduct each time you purchase a Trafford book, or make use of our publishing services. To find out how you are helping, please visit www.trafford.com/responsiblepublishing.html

Our mission is to efficiently provide the world's finest, most comprehensive book publishing service, enabling every author to experience success. To find out how to publish your book, your way, and have it available worldwide, visit us online at www.trafford.com/10510

 www.trafford.com

North America & international
toll-free: 1 888 232 4444 (USA & Canada)
phone: 250 383 6864 ♦ fax: 250 383 6804 ♦ email: info@trafford.com

The United Kingdom & Europe
phone: +44 (0)1865 722 113 ♦ local rate: 0845 230 9601
facsimile: +44 (0)1865 722 868 ♦ email: info.uk@trafford.com

10 9 8 7 6 5 4 3 2 1

Preface

Dedicated firstly & foremostly to my best friend "my mother"
To the "back four" Ian Williams, Carl Williams, Michelle Spencer, Matthew Ford
Gordan Taylor & Lyndsey Edwards (Tipton), George (whereas my seven iron) Graham Dave & Joan (Donnybrook Cork), Ronnie (get off of my cloud) McCloud, (Stornaway) Ian (Mitchells Bar Capetown), Derby Duck (Hamilton Bermuda).

The book was written whilst on board the Montrose, Beryl Alpha, Claymore, Piper Bravo,
Buzzard, Elgin, Franklin, Brent Delta & finished on the Amethyst, therefore it is appropriate to also specially dedicate to all the North Sea Tigers (past & present).

Please note that all events & characters depicted within this publication are fictitious.

1

Scorned Fury

1998 was a wonderful time of adventure for Jay, an ordinary working class man settling for the first time in another country, where not only the culture diverse to the one he had become used to, but also in certain quarters bigoted to his apparent lack of "political education" & social understanding of a political divide that had then lasted over eight hundred years.

Whilst arriving that day on the ferry, we were met at the ferryport by our representative Colm O'Sullivan, an unassuming middle aged gentleman with a softly spoken southern Irish accent, "and you must be the engineers from the U.K."

"Yes" replied Jay, his companion. Mel introduced himself, & both men were driven to the next village which is where they would make their home for the next eighteen months.

Whilst on the short picturesque journey, Jay absorbed the lush scenery while Mel talked to Colm of previous working experiences in the Irish Republic, mostly with fondness of apparent drunken debauchery on the subject of which Colm replied "would you like to sample a drop of the proper black stuff then", Mel like any non reformed alcoholic readily agreed, to which Jay was obviously outvoted & went with the spirit of the moment.

The Rebels Retreat was kind in hospitality & the black stuff flowed through the night like as if it cascaded freely from a waterfall. Mel exchanged his stories of the old country while Jay was mesmerised that evening by the beauty of one of the bar staff, an Irish coleen by the name of Franchesca. While Jay paid this beautiful lady unlimited compliments, Mel became increasingly worse for wear and Jay took the sensible step in getting Mel back to the home that had been given to them courtesy of their employers.

Several days passed & Jay having not forgotten the initial meeting with Franchesca popped his head around the door of the Rebels Retreat, to see if she was working that day & to his delight she was there. This time the gaze of eye contact was one that had to be broken by an additional member of staff with "are you not going to ask the man what he would like to drink Franchesca", "yes", replied Franchesca. Days, weeks & months passed by, the two lovers inseparable, but to the apparent distaste of Franchesca's father, a staunch Irish Republican with connections within the local Sinn Fienn organisation, to make matters worse he did not take too kindly to Jay who of British origin, being his daughter's lover.

Several years later, after marriage & the product of that marriage, a daughter born to the couple by the name of Victoria, much to the bigoted views of Brian, (Jays father in law), disgust, he seemed to think Jay had purposefully named his daughter Victoria after Queen Victoria to get his back up!, but Jay always strenuously denied this & their relationship became continuously strained.

One year on & a knock at the door, it was the Garda (Irish Police). "Franchesca Edwards", "yes" replied Franchesca, "Detective Inspector Murphy" & "Detective Sergeant Witty", "it's about your Dad Brian", "can we come in", "yes" replied Franchesca. What was about to be spelled out to Franchesca by the detectives was a huge shock to her system, "your father has been arrested on suspicion of rape with regards to your niece Sarah". Unbeknown to Jay was that Franchesca had been in a bitter feud with her father Brian who had threatened her with the Garda for innocently taking some photographs of baby Victoria in the bath, in her panic & lack of understanding she retaliated by spelling out her fears to a close friend, but also confided that she believed her father had been abusing her niece for some time & he should not be in any position to stand in judgement over a mother taking some innocent photographs of her daughter in the bath. What she had not calculated was her close friend reporting the matter to the Garda, this had now opened "a can of worms".

In the days & months into the investigation Jay's already strained relationship became even more strained with Franchesca's father Brian, who incidentally refuted & strenuously denied the allegations. Jay obviously over zealous due to the fact he had no reason to doubt his wife as he was so in love with her, also had no compassion towards a man who had been so bigoted & sectarian towards him since his association with his daughter.

Within a matter of time Brian was subsequently charged with raping Sarah, Franchesca became Public Enemy No 1 within her "own family", she was seen as the initiator after the Garda had threatened her with withholding evidence. Subsequently she made a statement & from this, other key witnesses were sourced & Brian eventually charged.

Franchesca's family bombarded her with threats, even resorting to violence & emotional blackmail, the emotional blackmail was in the shape & form of "if you testify against Dad, at seventy years of age, you will kill him".

Franchesca's state of mind was fragile as she was now in too deep to turn the clocks back, she could not either be seen to be a vindictive & scheming manipulator amongst friends & also family who were very dubious of the whole situation that had now spiralled out of control like a runaway train, who however was going to stop this loco as it steadily gathered momentum?

2

An isolated Franchesca was left in complete turmoil, with only her husband Jay as her "rock", family would constantly bombard her with threatening phone calls & the constant emotional blackmail now tugging at her heart strings like an elasticated band, stretched to almost breaking point. Jay continued his support as the dutiful husband, even though he was unaware of the tangled web of lies his wife had woven.

Franchesca started to drop hints that she would like a fresh start & move on outside of the Irish Republic, her motive very simple, she would not be made to testify against her father Brian, she also wanted a quick fix to a monster she had created but did not have any immediate answers.

Jay would apply in the interim period before Brian's trial at the Dublin Central Criminal Court for various positions overseas & it was not long before certain job offers were on the table, Hong Kong, the United States & Spain.

In the forthcoming weeks as Jay mulled over these offers, Franchesca wanted her own way & was adamant of the hotter climate of Spain's Costa del Sol had far more to offer, not quite the same remuneration package as the United States or Hong Kong, but Franchesca had her way & the move to Spain's Costa del Sol was underway, ironically as the move finalised, this was to be exactly six weeks before Brian's trial.

After Brian's trial & some months later Franchesca's family, not all, but some found it in their hearts with the Catholic faith to forgive, however Jay with no reason to ever doubt his wife whatsoever, did find it strange to say the least that the chain of communication resumed quite quickly after the trial with immediate family. Jay did not share the same sentiments, after all Brian to him was a paedophile & he could not bear the long distance calls to his wife from Brian & especially when Victoria was also speaking "to Grandad". This put an enormous strain on the relationship with constant rowing, Franchesca also found it difficult to adapt to the cultural diversity of the one she was now living in, this in turn gave her an alcohol dependency that was not known to Jay & in turn created more strain on the already now turbulent marriage.

The winter of the new Millennium was relatively short & sweet, by February that year Jay was told by his employers that the Company would be placed in administration, Jay would have to break the news to Franchesca who once informed would be less than enthusiastic about the change about to affect her current lifestyle. Franchesca was used to getting her own way, but destiny was about to teach her that she would have to take the rough with the smooth, several weeks on and the luxury apartment Jay shared with his wife had to be handed over & a return for Jay back to the British Islands was now imminent. The couple had ruled out a return back to the Irish Republic fearing there would be reprisals from family as Franchesca was a key witness in a trial she did not testify in, despite being made to feel welcome again by family after Brian's acquittal.

3

The return to the British Islands for Jay was a mixed bay of emotions, after all he had been an ex Pat for almost four years & had adhered to life outside of the U.K.

The border town of Wyevale had the backdrop of a picturesque elegance of an imaginary fairytale, however this would turn out to be no fairytale for Jay as Franchesca's chameleon character was about to unfold a change that Jay in time would never quite comprehend. Jay would have to pick projects up in various parts of the United Kingdom to give his cunning & devious wife the continued lifestyle she was now accustomed to, however what Jay did not realise was whilst the cat was away, the mouse would play, unbeknown to Jay his wife had embarked on a sordid lesbian liaison with her next door neighbour Mary an ex Metropolitan policewoman who had become embittered, due to the fact her high flying ex husband had dumped her & the children for another woman. Her hatred for men had changed her sexuality so much so she wanted to convert Franchesca's love of her husband into a love only shared for herself, for this she did achieve with some success. During months after the relationship grew stronger between the two women, Mary hatched a cunning plot that was to unfold to Jay with such conclusion that his marriage would collapse in a fashion reminiscent of the Berlin Wall.

Mary's plan entailed a former lesbian lover who she would ask a huge favour of, that favour was to seduce Jay, gather photographic evidence & post a letter with the photographs insisting that the individual in the photographs was someone who had been having an affair with Franchesca's husband for some time. This from Mary's point of view would be the straw that would break the camel's back & finally break Jay's marriage to Franchesca, thus driving Franchesca further into the arms of Mary her lesbian lover. Ironically Mary's former lover lived in the next village to where Jay was based in Chesterley, so logistically everything fell neatly into place for scheming Mary once she had stolen several photographs of Jay from her lover's home & subsequently scanned & e-mailed the photographs of Jay to her former lover. The plot was hatched & Abbey Lammerton an I.T. specialist & Mary's former lover, found it easy to go to Jay's hotel, subsequently seduce him and later entice him back to her home where being an I.T. specialist found it easy to download through hidden webcams sordid sexual acts between herself & Jay, thus putting the final pieces of her elaborate jigsaw together.

4

The plot now hatched & finalised unsuspecting Jay arrived home for a long weekend, whilst arriving back at the marital home, Jay had discovered the locks had been changed at the marital home in sleepy Wyevale, Mary however was delighted to inform Jay having spotted him pulling up in his car that Franchesca had gone away & was seeking a divorce due to his infidelity. Jay looked bewildered but Mary explained Franchesca was furious that she had received photographs of "his tart" & that a solicitor's letter had been forwarded to his mother's home.

Despite the resolution of complete defiance on Jay's face, Mary, a cunning & devious ex-Metropolitan policewoman would use every trick that she had cunningly learnt while having a secret admiration for corrupt policemen & women alike in her secret list for "bent" Met officers, however whilst these plans accumulated & gave birth to all the distaste & cunning elaborations that were about to unfold, Jay was as ever completely unexpecting of events that would unfold before him so explosively, that not even a cannon being fired in the rain would have such a force & shock value to one's system that this in itself would be testament to how this man's resolve would be ultimately "tested", & subsequent ultimate search for the truth. However that would be a long time for Jay to wait, however the taste of victory would be unbeknown to Jay & that much sweeter for a man who would flatly refuse to surrender in his ultimate quest for "justice", & so the table laid, only Jay knew his final thoughts of how he would exact the ultimate form of retribution, this however would be an after thought of what would be about to be cunningly "unleashed".

5

"woeful deceipt"

On a cold & rain swept January morning, Jay like any normal early morning routine placed his keys in his car door for the onward journey ahead, except this journey was a voyage of discovery of how a scorned woman would attempt to exact "her revenge" & stop at nothing to "level the series".

"Jay Edwards", "Detective Sergeant Ed Davids" & Detective Constable Ricky Lapland", "I am arresting you on suspicion of raping your wife Franchesca Edwards", as the rest of the caution was being read to Jay & as a result being placed in the back of a Police car, the sheer volume of unexpected events unfolding in front of Jay made him totally speechless during the short journey to Wyevale Police Station.

On arrival Jay still unable to comprehend what was happening to him, on arrival at sleepy Wyevale Police Station Jay asked the Custody Sergeant for legal representation, which was granted. Still reeling in shock, Jay's solicitor arrived some time later to brief Jay on the magnitude of what he was faced with, slowly but surely the penny had dropped & Jay's solicitor was the wake up call that Jay needed. However in a complex scenario it would take a big effort to finally piece this elaborate jigsaw together.

D.S Ed Davids & D.C. Ricky Lapland would go through the motions of cross examination in the presence of Jay's solicitor & after several days of intense questioning Jay was charged with raping his wife & now had to fight to clear that of his good name, although this would be made difficult due to the harsh bail conditions being imposed & movement restriction with regards to contacting anyone directly involved in the case.

Days, weeks passed by & Jay still unable to get to the bottom of the events that had now shattered his life, but still determined to get to the bottom of the web of lies that had been woven before him, one of the hardest things for Jay to accept was not being able to contact his beloved Victoria, this cut him like a knife.

Unbeknown to Jay in the weeks leading up to his wrongful arrest was that Mary who already had a platonic relationship with Ricky Lapland, had briefed Ricky Lapland with regards to Franchesca, ultimately this conspiracy to remove Jay out of Franchesca's life was simplified by the fact that Mary who knew

Ricky quite well from growing up in Wyevale was to call a "favour" in from past experience.

Once again Mary's cunning was to leave no stone unturned with regards to perverting the course of justice, Franchesca would be briefed once Mary had thrashed out the final details with Mary's plans coming to fruition. Franchesca was briefed to attend Wyevale Police Station on a specific time & day where Ricky Lapland would be "purposefully" hanging around the front desk, this would look then as though Ricky Lapland had just taken up the complaint.

Franchesca arrived as specified & Ricky Lapland followed the procedure of briefing his governor, Ed Davids that a lady had attended the front desk & had complained of being raped by her estranged husband, "shall I take this one Sarge", "yes" replied D.S Ed Davids, "but tread carefully with all that husband & wife stuff", "O.K. Sarge", replied Lapland.

Ricky arranged to interview Franchesca & took all the details of the complaint as pre-arranged, this in turn would go through all the protocol & procedure eventually leading to Jay's arrest. However what made matters more intense was after numerous interviews at length a certain chemistry had developed between Franchesca & Ricky which eventually became sexual. The bizarre love triangle could only become more detrimental to Jay's innocence, however because Ricky was now falling for Franchesca the complications that were in the making would obviously lead to mistakes being made by the co-conspirators.

6

"*Retribution*"

Jay now had to put together the "jigsaw", in an emotional rollercoaster Jay would find it difficult to remain focussed in the months leading up to his trial, however convinced of his innocence he would plot his revenge, as this was a monstrous betrayal kick started by a woman he once loved, that love now turned to sheer hatred, but Jay's plans were not to source retribution on the woman who was mother to Victoria, but to gain retribution on the people who conspired alongside Franchesca.

Once completely vindicated at Jay's trial, Jay would now elaborately plan the executions of Mary & Ricky Lapland, having been given vital information by another neighbour that Mary was Franchesca's lesbian lover & that she was also an ex Metropolitan Policewoman. Jay was also told that D.C. Ricky Lapland was also a secret lover of Franchesca, this ignited the flames of fury that now burned deep within Jay.

Jay needed a base not too far from Wyevale but also not too close, therefore the nearest city to Wyevale, Dewport about 20 miles west of Wyevale would be a perfect base for gathering intelligence and putting the final detailed plans together. Jay would learn to be patient in his quest for retribution.

How?, time?, place?, were the questions being asked in the back of Jay's mind. Jay would consult a former I.R.A. gun runner with whom he had worked alongside in the Irish Republic, as to carry out any executions he would need a weapon, Jay made contact with Billy Kelly a gun runner convicted for smuggling weapons from the United States to the Irish Republic, now reformed but still heavily connected to the old I.R.A. Jay was shown a secret arms cache that had been syphoned away by Kelly during the decommissioning process. After driving deep into the beautiful lush idyllic landscape of the Cork & Kerry mountains, Jay was to try out an array of weapons, however the field was narrowed down after hours of intense testing & firing to the AK47 & M16 with the M16 being the narrow victor with its specially adapted Henri Martini telescopic sights of which Kelly "threw in", at no extra cost. Jay once making the cash transaction with Kelly would visit a scrap dealer in Southern Ireland, his plan to enable him to smuggle the M16 out of the Republic. This would require him extracting the metal boot interior of a Series 5 B.M.W. identical to the one he owned, Jay would rent a garage nearby complete with compressor, he would then set about to modify the false boot interior and gradually shape it over the concealed weapon and its ammunition and countersink the modified section over the existing one through the fifth wheel space and once placed in position would fully weld the complete false interior and later prepare and respray the false boot interior internally and externally with identical colour coded matches to mask the penetrative fusion of the modified boot interior in the event of the vehicle being searched.

With the formality of a successful crossing back to the mainland Jay would continue his plans with full vigour.

Jay next had to come up with Plan B (the assassination time & place).

First he would need to gather intelligence on Ricky Lapland, as for Mary he knew she had not moved from the house next to Franchesca's, so additional information on Lapland would in essence be a premium. Whilst staying in the Dewport area Jay as if by a stroke of magic had a great slice of luck, as whilst out one evening in Dewport in a wine bar he was drawn to a very elegant & vivacious looking woman who was alone at the bar & after a formal introduction of both parties exchanging compliments it was not long before both parties had discovered what vocation in life they were, Jay the engineer & luckily for Jay this beautiful woman was an Information Technology specialist working at the Police headquarters in Dewport. This area covered Wyevale, Jay now had to somehow get the exact whereabouts of Lapland without raising suspicion, for this Jay would initially play the part of the complete gentleman & wait for fresh ideas with regards to diplomatically extracting the required information out of this beautiful young lady who worked at Police H.Q.

Paula Kempton was Jay's answer to the exact location of Ricky Lapland, however patience would triumph over all else in later gathering vital information on Lapland.

Several weeks later after continued compliments, romantic meals & flowers, Jay came up with a host of ideas, however in the interim period Paula had now fallen head over heels in love with Jay (as Jay had wanted), so now was the right time to hatch the best of ideas. Jay would tell Paula that between contracts he would work freelance as a debt recovery specialist, to convince Paula he would show her a business card he had got printed at a motorway service station with his name printed on this card with his secondary & fictitious vocation. Also highlighted, he had also fictitiously printed himself a list of names of individuals that were living in the Dewport area including Laplands that had disappeared off the electoral register & were priorities for debt recovery, so Jay asked the question, "Paula I've got a guy here that has disappeared off the face of the earth", owing vast amounts of money & has quite a bonus attached to him if I can establish his whereabouts", "Could you gather any information on this chap at work", "I know you are not supposed to", "but this guy is probably a criminal anyway", "so look at it as doing his victims a favour", Paula replied, "You're asking a lot", "I know", replied Jay "but if you don't want to help me honey I will understand", putting his arm around her & kissing her on the cheek as he reassured her, after a tender embrace, Paula said "So what is this guy's name", Jay playing down the whole situation pretended he did not recollect the person he required the information on, and went to look through the fictitious names & even pretended to look through the list, "ah yes here he is", stated Jay, "a Ricky Lapland, last living in the Dewport area", "OK" replied Paula, "Just leave it there for the morning", "and I will take it with me to work", "but this is a one off", "I understand honey", replied Jay.

The following evening Paula met Jay at her home stated there were several people R. Lapland in the Dewport area of which she passed the addresses on to Jay, she also stated & laughed one of these guys is an acting Police officer in the country of Dewport, "so I doubt very much if it's one of our own", "Yes", replied Jay containing his excitement, Ricky Lapland's location was now established, Jay would now plot his execution & after carrying out various surveys of Lapland's movements, Jay would elaborately plan not only the execution but the quick successive secondary execution of Mary, for this, timing was of the essence & to make good his escape Jay would disguise himself as a "typical" civil servant or "sales" type dying his hair black & donning a pair of National Health glasses. With this Jay would once again get fictitious business cards printed & masquerade as a freelance insurance salesman.

His sales pitch would not be overpowering but subtle in the sense that he would tell those individuals adjacent to Lapland's home that there was no obligation to commit to any purchases, however they would be allowed to enter a free prize draw & one couple in particular would be selected not too far from Lapland & told within weeks that they were the lucky winners of an exclusive 4 day break to Paris, an all expenses paid trip that would be booked several months in advance from the time the lucky recipients were given the good news. This in essence would give Jay the required time scale to add the finishing touches to his elaborate planning, Jay being the engineer would calculate in triangulation formulae the exact distance of angle & bearing from Lapland's house to the recipients of the exclusive 4 day break in Paris. A time & day would now be selected with timing being the most important attribute. Once the escape route established, Mary was to be the final target. For this Mary's movements were carefully analyzed & by now Jay had decided to kidnap Mary & take her to an apartment nearby where a makeshift scaffold was to be erected inside complete with trap door, with Jay having an eye for the ladies he guessed Mary was an average size 12 to 14, so his calculations of average weight to ratio would be calculated & certain tests therefore would be carried out to ensure Mary's final resting place would be her resting place from the make shift gallows that were now erected in the temporary apartment Jay now rented. However he wanted to leave his mark on Wyevale & decided that a proportion of concrete floor would be removed and the mobile scaffold centralised between floor joists so that Mary's body would fall through into the apartment below, even in the event of Mary putting on weight, Jay had left nothing to chance & even placed two hydraulic rams between the joists so that there was plenty of tolerance between the joists when Mary fell for the last time, this would be the shock value that Jay would leave on the unexpecting neighbours in the apartment below. After this he too would become part of the pact by executing himself with a 2.2 calibre Colt diamond back, ironically this was the first gun Jay had fired in his life & fittingly he wanted to leave this world with it being the last he would fire.

Now with the finishing touches being put to his plan of retribution Jay needed to practice his target skills with the M16 he had purchased from Kelly the former convicted gun runner, however he would need to discover a location where suspicion would not be drawn towards him, for this he would finally decide to combine a holiday with target practice, as this would be his last holiday after all, so where then in the world could Jay go to practice with a M16, eventually the answer was quite simple, (Vietnam). For years since the repatriation of Vietnam, tourists were given the opportunity to get to use assault rifles such as the AK47 & the M16, so this was perfect for Jay, as not only would he get to practice everyday but would also be able to fire at different angles, the same as the triangulation formulae he had calculated for the first "hit" on Ricky Lapland. This would be carried out once the lucky recipients of the four day break were away in Paris so that Jay could gain access to their home whilst they were away for the first of the executions. Jay after days of practice would put the finishing touches to his target skills, taking in the wonderful sights & culinary delights of Saigon one week before he was due to fly back to the United Kingdom.

However Jay would be taken with his roving eye yet again, this time it would be a Communist party worker selling propaganda from the Vietnam war. Qyuen was a vivacious looking woman with a smile as wide as the Mekong Delta. Those qualities would quite obviously impress Jay who would strike up conversation whilst still engaged in full eye contact & that eye contact would lead to Jay asking the final of many questions that afternoon, that question being, "I understand Saigon can be quite a vibrant &

intoxicating city", "providing you have got the right type of guide", the penny now dropped & Qyuen now as red as the Communist party flag that predominantly & proudly hung from the wall of the propaganda memorabilia that she sold would pull herself together for that brief moment with, "And do you think that I am the right sort of guide Ahh Mr Sorry", "Jay Edwards", "Just call me Jay", with the foundations of this relationship cemented a table for two was booked at the Caravelle in central Saigon, Jay would however concentrate on an emotional detachment that would not blind his vision of months & months of elaborate planning & look upon this as a holiday romance without any emotion & fun for the last time in his chequered life.

The table set at the Caravelle Jay ever the gentleman knowing he would have to remain detached, but still enjoy the last moments & weeks of his life, paid Qyuen unlimited compliments during a very pleasant evening, that would transpire late on into the following day. As the rising sun shone purposefully in the bright Saigon sky, Jay turned to Qyuen & realised he had not rudely woken from some broken dream, for this was so surreal.

With the genuine demeanour of Qyuen & that vibrancy driving home to Jay even further, Jay with an almost instant attraction that was trying its best to place itself under Jay's skin, was for the this time in his life attempting to remain emotionally detached from the elaborate planning that had completely taken over his life. Still he believed he could emotionally detach himself, however the last week would seem like and eternity & despite Jay wanting the emotional detachment he found it hard to ignore the charms & elegance of this beautiful young lady.

The bright city lights of Saigon were not the only thing that shone so vibrantly that evening, for Jay despite his promise to himself of emotional detachment it was becoming more & more difficult to keep the distance required between his elaborate plans & this beautiful young lady & her intoxicating charms ever more apparent.

The clock now ticking, Jay wanted this clock to wind down quicker than ever considering Qyuen was slowly but surely getting under Jay's skin.

The second morning of togetherness brought a ray of light Jay did not want to be accustomed to, however he believed he could now get close & still carry out his months & months of elaborate planning. Every second & every day of Jay's last days in Saigon were cherished & respected, however time passes by so much quicker in the perfect spirit of the moment for Qyuen, however Jay now a mixed bag of emotions was finding the time was dragging by more so than it normally would due to the intoxicating aroma of this beautiful woman & his final solution to the elaborate planning of ultimate retribution that was now underway, so Jay would temporarily suspend his most inner feelings & enjoy the spirit of the moment with this enchanting young lady. "So what would you like to do next", Jay asked Qyuen, "I don't care what I do next", "I just want to spend my time with you", "Sounds quite good to me", replied Jay, with all the armour plating Jay had placed around himself he could not but like this woman despite his ever now determined efforts to keep her out of his heart, however he was not the ordinary loner type of guy living in his own little world for what had sparked something inside this quite pleasant & charming young man was in certain terms an unforgiving betrayal that would obviously leave its mark deep inside Jay, however would & could love triumph over evil?

7
The Final Countdown

The last twenty four hours of togetherness brought a tense climax to what Jay could only see as the "inevitable", so Jay would masquerade to Qyuen that nothing was wrong as she could now undoubtedly feel Jay's tension building because she had been so close, sensually & sexually that she could sense something was wrong, however when she confronted Jay with this obvious tension that surrounded her confused feelings like some kind of Masonic handshake shrouded in secrecy, she wanted to dig deeper but knew now that time was of the essence & decided to enjoy every last hour without wasting the last moments on something for now she could not unravel.

The short journey to the airport in the morning was a mixed bag of emotional turmoil with Qyuen wondering if she would ever see the man she had now fallen in love with & Jay was also feeling indifferent in the sense that he knew his elaborate planning would bring the curtain down on the final chapter of his life but was feeling confused despite the distance he had attempted to place between him & Qyuen and of course months upon months of elaborate planning, momentarily Jay would switch off for the tender & beautiful moments now being shared with Qyuen.

The outbound journey now set & Jay airborne, the impression that Qyuen had left, whether it was to be everlasting only time could now be judge & jury over this.

Jay's arrival back in the United Kingdom was the reality check he needed as this wake up call would not come between his sworn revenge & the tenderness shared with Qyuen, that reality check being a typical rain swept cold morning on arrival in the British Islands. Now it was time to put everything together & bring all of the planning to a conclusion.

Jay had left nothing to chance and had hatched a contingency plan in the unlikely event of any plans being scuppered after extracting some time before handing the M16 out of the boot of the Series five, he had hidden the high powered assault rifle & its ammunition away from the apartment he had temporarily leased and would take the weapon 24 hours from its secondary hide out before Ricky Lapland's execution. Jay had been quite elaborate when it came to the alternative "hide out" for the M16 before extracting it from the false boot interior, Jay had logistically analyzed the terrain of the Wyevale river and its embankments, quite advantageously the river had quite a substantial rise and fall of tide, Jay again being the engineer had manufactured a pressurised cylinder to place the weapon and its ammunition in this air tight cylinder, after carefully scrutinising the embankments along the river bank Jay had decided that if the cylinder was to be placed in the river then it would be somewhere where it would be almost impossible for any boat to moor alongside where the cylinder would be anchored to the river bed.

For this a medieval castle stood proudly & purposefully practically perpendicular with the cliff face to the west side of the river, this would allow Jay to abseil in the dead of the night whilst anchored from the ruin complete with diving suit into the Wyevale river, whilst still attached by his cows tails to his descender and shunt this in itself would compensate for the strong currents from time to time by still being attached to the descender and shunt. The cylinder that Jay had manufactured was unique in design in that it consisted of two parts both of which were cylindrical & of the same diameter. The top section housed the assault rifle & the detachable bottom section was hollow as the top section except there was a valve fitted so that when it made contact with the water after Jay's descent, Jay would open the valve to fill the bottom section with water this being attached to a secondary line, thus once filled to capacity would automatically sink itself & mechanically anchor itself to the river bed. With the upper part of the cylinder still being pressurised

Jay had calculated "the weight to ratio" to sink the two sectioned cylinder and for it to be mechanically anchored to the river bed until it was ready to be detached for the sole purpose, that being the ultimate execution of Lapland.

With everything planned to the very last detail Jay would now within the last twenty four hours before Lapland's execution take time for reflection, to remain totally focussed and emotionally detached Jay would listen to classical Wagner, the classical masterpieces would psychologically make him focus for all the pre planning that had been put together over months & months of elaborate disciplines & thoughts. With the lucky recipients of the exclusive four day break now in Paris Jay would proceed as pre planned to enter their home now complete with the M16 in semi automatic mode & the Colt diamond back 2.2 hand gun to his vantage point, why at almost a 45 degree angle? The answer was quite simple as the escape route was more feasible & closer to an adjacent field, now patiently awaiting for Lapland to appear to make his way to work, soon it would shortly conclude, just as Jay had planned, a small piece placed into an elaborate jigsaw, nothing now could possibly go wrong, or could it?, the moment of truth was now unfolding as the front door to Lapland's home was opened, Jay would wait until Lapland would as judged by previous surveys, place his keys into his car for the onward journey, the last journey of Lapland's life, however Lapland's wife would follow behind Lapland holding a child in her arms unfortunately for Jay & uncharacteristically Ricky's wife was holding Jay's daughter in her arms as she followed Ricky out to his parked car for her & Victoria to wave Ricky off to work. This was not how Jay had wanted this to end as he could not execute Lapland in front of his beloved Victoria, he had no idea that Ricky's wife who could not have any children had offered to baby sit that previous evening for Franchesca & Mary to have a night of lesbian indulgence, however for Jay the months upon months of elaborate planning had been ruined by virtue of the fact Ricky's wife was left holding the baby, that baby was of course Jay's beloved Victoria. Emotionally now drained & tearful Jay sat slumped with assault rifle and left feeling "humanised" at visualising Victoria at the intended assassination vantage point. Would & could Jay ever build up again to yet another such emotional & powerful anti climax?

Several days later Jay had retreated back to the home he had temporarily rented, feeling tired & emotionally drained, he would carefully reflect & gather his thoughts over the next couple of days. The high powered assault rifle could not be left at the apartment he had temporarily rented, after careful reflection he had decided to dismantle the weapon, hacksaw the barrel complete with firing mechanism into handful proportions & with the use of oxygen & acetylene smelt what was left of the evidence into non existence, this was decided after carefully considering that to go back to the original "dive" site & reload the pressurised cylinder, reweight it and reinstate it at the bottom of the Wyevale river was too dangerous & despite months upon months of elaborate planning the "show would go on".

As the weeks passed by Jay was coming up with fresh ideas yet again despite the efforts that had been unrewarded to a man who had initially decided on the ultimate form of retribution, he had been left feeling "humanised", after visualising Victoria unwittingly at the intended assassination site, therefore he would elaborate upon numerous ideas, & felt that despite being of non religious denomination, he did feel that what was meant to happen was in fact meant to happen, in this instance he would revert to Plan B and that would mean making Lapland & Mary's life as miserable as he possibly could without the necessity of murder.

8

The Best Laid Plans

For all the planning & logistical whereabouts of Mary & Ricky Jay had many distinctive advantages as by now he had gathered an exhaustive amount of information on the intended victims, so he would now keep it simple after all Mary had been exceptionally devious when destroying Jay's marriage to Franchesca with her friend Abbey Lammerton the I.T. specialist.

Jay decided to initiate things, he would employ a private investigator firstly to dig dirt on Mary & secondly to dig dirt on Ricky, as he already knew and had unravelled the long underlying deceit which clearly boiled now well above the surface. Rather than recruit somebody locally with regards to giving him information he already knew, he needed somebody at least several counties away from the individuals he intended to gather intelligence upon, firstly because of Mary's former colleagues & knowledge of officers within the local Constabulary & the fact that a lot of retired Police officers took up the vocation of a private investigator after leaving the Police force. With no stone unturned Jay still being "driven", decided whilst on a business trip to seek the advice of a former Detective Chief Superintendent of Cleverland Constabulary after an extensive search through certain directories & basic interview techniques over the telephone with regards to recruiting the right person. For this specific task, Jay after extensively interviewing a number of people decided that Brian Lawson was indeed the man for the required tasks, the "gut instinct" in Jay left him in no doubt that Brian was the man for the job, after agreeing to meet Brian at a motorway service station, Jay outlined the information that he required on Ricky & Mary.

Firstly Brian would gather evidence on Ricky & Franchesca, this would be enough to supply Ricky's long suffering wife with everything Jay wanted her to be supplied with, i.e. photographs concluding intimate embraces, these photographs together with recorded phone calls would not only give the required & desired effect on Ricky's marriage, but also the desired effect on Franchesca's lesbian relationship with Mary, as photographs would be supplied to an unexpected Mary of Franchesca's sexual acts of betrayal with Ricky, but also the second set of photographs supplied to Ricky's wife Veronica, this would seem to kill two birds with one stone in the initiation of a new kind of retribution going to be "dished" out to the unexpected recipients. Jay of course acquiring the services of Brian Lawson the ex super cop, would not only remain discreetly out of "the picture", but knew Brian with all his impeccable background & character would be sure that discretion would be of paramount importance to his clientele & the services they required, so as expected Brian delivered all the evidence within weeks of his investigation, Jay now armed with the required information, supplied firstly Ricky's wife Veronica with the photographs of Ricky's infidelity with Franchesca. Once again Jay had disguised himself when ensuring to call when Ricky had gone to work with all the evidence, however he said that he had been employed as a private investigator with a tangled & messy custody battle over Mary's children by her ex husband, knowing the relationship with Mary & Franchesca & certain incidents that were occurring within that relationship may be supportive to his client's custody battle. With this Veronica fell hook line & sinker for the script that was being given to her by a well disguised Jay, with prior knowledge of the friendship between Ricky, Veronica, Mary & Franchesca, Jay could now sit back & see their relationships nose dive in a web of deceit, lies & dishonesty that surely had run its course, however unbeknown to Jay was that Veronica, Ricky's wife had some history with depression, anxiety & suicidal psychological disorders & this was to have a devastating effect on a conclusion that Jay had never comprehended or envisaged ever ending the way in which it was about to. Despite having plotted the ultimate form of retribution Jay without realising had woken a sleeping giant in Wyevale, that sleeping giant was of course Veronica Lapland. Now Veronica was to be an unknown quantity with regards to her now own sense of betrayal, Jay just thought after his traumatic roller coaster ride with regards to his emotional turmoil that Veronica would go down the usual avenues of divorce, financial settlements, etc, how further from the truth could he be & not having any idea of Veronica Lapland's fragile state of mind & previous psychological disorders.

That afternoon Veronica now an emotional wreck drank consistently as she awaited for Ricky to alight from his car as he arrived home, without delay Ricky walked into the living room of the marital home to discover Veronica in less than a good mood, "what's wrong Veronica", "why do you look so sad", clutching at an A4 size brown envelope Veronica emptied its contents on to the coffee table & to Ricky's horror he now realised that someone had been playing the part of shall we say a better detective than what he had. Now speechless & dumbfounded he reached out to touch his wife, the pain & anguish now transparent in Veronica's eyes said it all, his wife pushed Ricky away insisting "don't touch me you bastard", Ricky sensed the vibrancy of unwelcome so much so he retreated sensibly to the kitchen puzzled & baffled he stared hopelessly into space not comprehending the magnitude of hurt he had unleashed on his long suffering wife. As he quickly loosened his tie to take a deeper than normal breath of fresh air he felt a jolt of cold steel plunder into his lower back, as he turned to face Veronica he realised he had been stabbed by his wife, reeling now in pain he attempted to place his hands on Veronica in a vain attempt to stop her, however his efforts were considerably slower because of the shock at being stabbed & so Veronica repeatedly continued where she had left off repeatedly stabbing Ricky as that last gasp of air happened to be the last of his life slumped hopelessly on the floor & without even a second thought Veronica now like a woman possessed calmly wiped the 8" kitchen knife of her now late husband's blood with a kitchen towel & placed it in her handbag picking Ricky's car keys up, she casually walked to the front door. As she calmly closed it behind her, her neighbour who had obviously overheard a "domesticated situation", asked "are you O.K. Veronica", "yes no problem Ricky is just being an arsehole yet again", with an apprehensive smile from the neighbour, Veronica's demeanour was less than shall we say casual, however she proceeded to place the car keys in the door of her late husband's car & proceeded to the home she knew all too well that home being the home where Mary & Franchesca shared.

So cool calm & collected she had now taken a controlled grip on her emotions as she proceeded in the short journey she knew all too well. As luck would have it Franchesca was in the house she shared with Mary all alone. As Franchesca opened the door Veronica asked, "is Mary at home Franchesca", "no she has taken the kids to her Mum's", we are having a quiet night in just the two of us", "come on in Veronica she will be back soon", "do you fancy a cuppa Veronica", "that would be nice Fran", as Franchesca proceeded to the kitchen, Veronica soon followed she had taken the 8" kitchen knife from her handbag and formatted an identical assault on Franchesca as previously carried out on her late husband, although Franchesca slumped almost immediately to the floor, she slightly turned to face Veronica realising the stab wound could be fatal she realised by the look of anger & anguish that Veronica knew that she had been uncovered with regards to her liaisons with Ricky, for the moment she was speechless, then standing unexpectedly behind Veronica was Mary having returned & stumbled across a scene that was reminiscent to a horror movie. Whilst containing her emotions for a woman she loved, she had to draw upon the training that she had received in the Met with such high powered emotive scenarios. "Veronica I know you're hurting", "please talk to me, don't hurt Franchesca any more", Veronica now turned to face Mary & replied, "don't you know that your girlfriend has been fucking my Ricky", Franchesca now heavily losing a lot of blood replied in a faint & struggled speech, "don't listen to her, she's a liar Mary", with this & Veronica now facing Mary looked deep into Mary's eyes, Mary now realised that she had to make her move or risk possible death & so with this ultimatum in the back of her mind, she lunged forward clasping both hands around the sharp instrument of terror now predominantly in the hands of a woman who had lost all sense of reason. As a violent struggle ensued, Fran had managed to pick herself up as the women struggled violently to take control of the situation & with one last gasp Franchesca had picked up an iron & struck Veronica as hard as she could over the back of her head despite clutching her wound with one hand, Veronica fell in a downward motion whilst still on top of Mary, unconscious and falling to the ground. An unconscious Veronica unwittingly with her weight on top of Mary whilst both women hit the floor simultaneously the knife that had been so fiercely fought for plunged directly and tragically through Mary's heart. Within minutes Mary had died from the fatal stab wound, Franchesca now traumatised and semi conscious was greeted by the emergency services & rushed to hospital, along with Veronica. Suddenly the scene became so surreal with Police, & eventually media, Jay unbeknown to him had placed the television on that same evening to his amazement to discover the "horror" & its extent unfolding never could he have ever envisaged the plot ending the way he wanted it to originally end but "totally unplanned", his immediate thoughts now were for his beloved Victoria firmly in the back of his mind.

Franchesca laid up in hospital the following morning with her injuries critical, but not life threatening, while Jay had now gone into a tangent with regards to Victoria & to seize upon an opportunity to be reunited with her, however he had decided to play a low key affair with regards to reinstating his vested interest with regards to his beloved Victoria. However he had contacted the local Social Services within a week as the opportunity was too good to resist & through the correct channels Jay would see his beloved Victoria once again and felt that "justice" had been seen to have been served with regards to Ricky & Mary but in a way he could never ever have envisaged. Finally in the weeks after the killings Veronica was charged with two counts of murder, Franchesca was finally released from hospital, Jay resumed regular contact with Victoria & his relationship reignited with Quyen he had learned to love again, but not only that, he had learned to forgive & forget.

9
Final Chapter

Life had new meaning, Jay had suffered at the hands of the conspirators who conspired in his downfall, but in the end justice had been seen to have been served, but with some kind of divine intervention, or had it? The tabloid press had covered the story quite extensively, Veronica Lapland had given a description of the man who had called at her home that fateful morning to the Police, but Jay Edwards had been quite elusive with his disguise, and had even disguised his accent with that of a broad Belfast accent, so considering Veronica already knew Jay she could never have fathomed out who the real individual was under that elaborate disguise that had supplied her with all the evidence of Ricky's infidelity that had unintentionally pushed her over the edge, furthermore Wyevale Constabulary were baffled as to who the individual was who had supplied Veronica with all the evidence of Detective Lapland's infidelity to an unsuspecting wife, as there were no prints from the photographs & brown A4 size envelope that had housed the incriminations of Ricky's deceit, Jay had been elaborate to say the least as not to handle anything that would link him to the crime scene as he had not directly handled anything incriminating that was handed to him by investigator Lawson also when invited into Veronica's home after again producing yet another fictitious card this time masquerading for his third & final fictitious vocation as private investigator he had been careful as not to handle any contents that were handed to Veronica on initially being invited into her home as he had worn drivers gloves whilst handling the evidence and sensibly took them off when sitting down to avoid any suspicion being cast in his direction & even placed them back on when leaving as not to provoke any further suspicion as the morning air had been brisk and cold to say the least. Brian Lawson however had attempted to contact Jay as he too had seen the horror unfolding on national television and with Brian's clean cut impeccable former background wanted to believe he had not been involved in anything underhanded to say the least, so Jay had answered Brian's call in an attempt to avoid suspicion by stating he was acting for a third party & innocently handed the photographs to a third party who he was not prepared to name, Brian however remained sceptical to say the least as he had not made it in his former vocation as a D.C.I. by being naïve, but would also weigh up anything that may or may not incriminate him in what was now deemed by himself as complex to say the least. In the months leading up to Veronica Lapland's trial she had adhered to prison life with her previous medical history now justifying her medication being supplied by the prison medic, and to make life that trifle more bearable, the prison Governor Sue Haymen who unbeknown to Veronica was a closet lesbian who had subsequently taken a shine to Veronica & subsequently recommended that she work as a trustee as Governor Haymen's personal assistant whilst incarcerated at Gladstonville Women's Prison. Governor Haymen had been promoted to Governor for over a year & had tread on a lot of toes to get to where she was amongst the high echelons of penal reform, Haymen a non graduate but smooth operator had manipulated everything in her wake to satisfy her egotistical persona by even carrying out sexual favours along the way in her labyrinth of social climbing & manipulation, so an unexpecting Veronica would be no match for Governor Haymen considering she had lived a sheltered life despite her medical history as Ricky's long suffering wife. However Veronica was not about to question anything that was making the living hell of two counts of murder hanging over her bearable to say the least. Regular visits to Gladstonville Women's Prison by Veronica's defence team headed by Carla Williams a specialist Q.C. specialising in cases involving abused women who subsequently killed, however Veronica had killed twice, both premeditated and so it was decided given the medical history that a plea of not guilty to two counts of murder and guilty to manslaughter on the grounds of diminished responsibility would be the best option and way forward with of course an adjournment for psychiatric reports, however Carla Williams with the class & distinction that undoubtedly made her one of Great Britain's finest barristers of her generation would play the part of the realist & give Veronica the reality check that would awaken her to the enormity of what she was faced with, that she could be convicted in front of a jury &

that the plea of diminished responsibility may not be accepted, so Veronica shell shocked after a legal visit by the charismatic Carla bid her farewells to her impressive defence team, and retreated back to her incarcerated surroundings with the help of a prison officer oblivious to the enormity & psychological uncertainty that now unhinged in the back of Veronica's ever fragile state of mind.

So back at the wing Veronica reported back to Governor Haymen with a knock upon that of Governor Haymen's door, "come in", "Ahh Lapland so how did your legal visit go", well not too good Miss Haymen, my barrister Carla has told me there are no guarantees, with this Veronica began to break down & cry, even with the medication now being prescribed the enormity & reality of what Carla had discussed had begun to dig deep into the resolve of even a medicated & tranquillised Veronica, despite her self esteem being at an all time low, Governor Haymen manoeuvred herself from around the desk & placed her arms in a passionate embrace around a woman she was clearly fond of with the reassurance of "try to relax Lapland" "try not to worry", with that Sue stood behind Veronica & started to massage that of her neck & shoulder muscles, suddenly all the burdens of the weights world upon Veronica's shoulders started to ebb & ease away like a castaway lost at sea. "That is so nice Miss Haymen", replied Veronica, "for the time being you can call me Sue", "and I in turn will call you Veronica", with that statement Sue began to unbutton Veronica's blouse, a sense of venture into the unknown for Veronica but also a sense of freedom now in the back of Veronica's mind as she had never been caressed by another woman with such sensitive eroticism, Sue continued to undress

Veronica and Veronica's voyage of discovery with her new found sexuality had begun, Sue took the dominant lead while Veronica now laid across Governor Haymen's desk moaning and groaning in apparent ecstasy as Sue manoeuvred her tongue expertly over the most smallest and sensitive details of Veronica's body with such precision even a Field Marshall would have been proud of such skilful manoeuvres, both women now wrapped around each other's bodies, and for Veronica her voyage of discovery had been one of high octane eroticism, that she now regretted she had not indulged earlier in her life as a multiple orgasm was something she had never had the pleasure of experiencing during her long suffering marriage to Ricky, as she got up to get dressed Sue placed her hand on Veronica's face and with a tender kiss she whispered into that of her lover's ear "that was nice", Veronica replied "the feeling's mutual", a chemistry had developed, a surprising and unexpected chemistry to say the least as both women now sent their pulses racing, a dangerous liaison had now developed, because stolen moments for the lovers was all they shared in the incarcerated surroundings of Gladstonville.

The weeks passed by and the bonding between Sue & Veronica became deeper & stronger, for Sue however it was becoming difficult to say the least when returning home as the emptiness of her bed and the longing to be with her lover coupled with the fact that the forbidden fruits she now shared with Veronica could lead to her downfall & subsequently end her self manufactured high standing position within Gladstonville if uncovered by Home Office officials, needless to say Sue weighed up the odds that were stacked against the longing to be with someone of the same sex who pushed all the right buttons for her even considering Veronica had been a recent convert to the art form of lesbianism, for Veronica it too was starting to feel the same after she too felt the longing to be with her lover during her isolation of the four grey walls that evidently surrounded her.

Within several weeks Veronica would be given a date in which to enter her plea, that plea on the sound advice of Carla Williams would be not guilty to the murders of late husband Ricky Lapland and not guilty to the murder of Mary Murphy, but guilty to the manslaughter on both counts on the grounds of diminished responsibility, and then obviously an adjournment for psychiatric reports to be submitted to support that of Veronica's plea, Sue was given all the details by her lover as and when it came in from her lover Veronica, now in too deep, Governor Haymen did not want the love she shared to end & therefore with a conclusion now imminent, even if a jury accepted her pleas & convicted her of manslaughter, a lengthy prison sentence would still be inevitable, so the thoughts of the forbidden fruits now shared by the two women coming to an abrupt ending was now apparently unimaginable and with that in her mind, Sue was now seriously contemplating an escape plan, she never thought she would ever feel this way over a woman, as her career had always come first, however love had now for the first time in her life had completely taken over everything in her wake as she now did not want anything to interrupt or spoil the intimacy that they had so tenderly shared.

Although she had not discussed the prospect of escape with her lover, Sue first wanted to carry out the feasibility study of escape knowing that she was the most powerful person in

Gladstonville, and so therefore access & egress to restricted areas would therefore not be a problem, however she would elaborate in her mind now the clock was ticking with regards to Veronica's forthcoming trial.

Her brother David a British National living in Northern Cyprus, she would consult assistance from, after all she could trust David with anything as they were so close when growing up, and Sue was also Godmother to David's son, she had also been there for him during his marriage break up to Katrina and would therefore call a favour or two in, David had not exactly been the black sheep in the Haymen family but had accumulated a fortune from suspect time shares, so Sue knew that David could probably sort a lot of things out with his underworld connections, and with regular contact with her beloved brother she would make her proposals to David as she knew he would be visiting the UK on business that same week and subsequently arranged to meet him at a hotel nearby where he would be entertaining prospective clients with his impressive portfolio of property time shares.

Sue had taken a photograph with that of her mobile phone of her lover Veronica and without confiding her plans, she stated to Veronica that she wanted to be reminded of her lover when away from the surreal surroundings of Gladstonville, however her motive was one which was dissimilar to what she had discussed with Veronica, as to what she would now discuss with her meeting with David, so as pre planned the meeting took place and once the family embraces and pleasantries were exchanged, Sue began to discuss her inner plans to David, David was very sceptical to say the least, but Sue begged him to help, and therefore after several hours of pleas, David realising that his beloved sister was hopelessly in love, he reluctantly gave assurances that he would assist in Sue's bid for Veronica's freedom.

So Sue explained she would require David's assistance with regards to cloning a new identity & therefore after an extensive search in the prison archives, the name of Maria Stanovich a prisoner of eastern European origin would be the ideal candidate for Veronica to clone that of her identity, and therefore the digital images that had been captured were handed to David along with Maria Stanovich's date of birth & next of kin details for the cloning of that identity, David already stated he had someone in mind that could clone the digital image with that of all the details supplied alongside all the information with that of a bona fide validated E.U. passport.

With David's all but reluctant agreement to assist his sister in Veronica's escape bid, it was now down to Sue to concentrate on that of the finer details of the escape bid, despite Veronica's appearance being completely different to that of her lover's this could have some distinctive advantages as Sue with the 1960 style black bob haircut and square cut designer glasses could concentrate on donning her identity on that of Veronica's, her basic plan she envisaged would firstly be to convince Veronica to participate in her plans with of course the prize ultimately being that both lovers be united in freedom, she had envisaged a daring escape plan providing Veronica adhered to the simplicity of Sue's plans which entailed taking her hostage for her to make good of that of her escape, Sue Haymen realised that if Veronica kept her nerve there was a better than average chance of a successful escape plan coming to a dramatic conclusion in the favour of the two lovers, and so with this in mind Sue decided that after more stolen moments of lesbian indulgence she popped the question to Veronica in a roundabout way with, "Darling do you envisage this ever ending because I don't want this to end", No I suppose not replied Veronica, "but I worry that when I am convicted, we will be separated", "I have given this some serious thought & I too don't want this to end either" replied Sue, "however if you adhere to my plans then you could be free with my assistance". "You are saying that I escape", yes replied Sue as she gave Veronica a reassuring embrace, Veronica did not need to be asked twice as she readily agreed to the escape plan & so both lovers plotted all details and even bounced different idealisms with regards to the escape plot.

Sue had explained that her brother David was preparing a new identity with regards to false E.U. documentation & supporting E.U. passport. She also explained that they would have to lay low if the escape bid was successful after the fallout of the escape from Home Office officials, she explained she would purchase a different phone when dealing with David at his request so that no calls could be monitored in the aftermath of the subsequent escape & knowing full well she would be a prime suspect with not only the Police but also the Home Office, she explained to Veronica that discipline would be the key & patience if the lovers would be reunited & so they both agreed to stick by all the plans that they now conspired to fulfilment, the basic plan would be for Veronica to disguise herself as Governor Haymen after of course Sue had been tied up and made to look as though she had been taken hostage with a window of opportunity of at least one hour to make good that of her departure from these islands with David's help before the escape was "uncovered" and so emphasis was placed on the timing of the escape, Sue already had a 1960 black bob wig which she had kept in her wardrobe after she had shaved all her hair off for a charity event some time back for the local community which would be significant in Veronica's bid for freedom as well as the square cut designer glasses which would be taken from her during Veronica's attempt at freedom, secondly there were three keys in total that would lead to Veronica's freedom, firstly the wing in which untried prisoners like Veronica were housed, secondly the main reception area and finally the gate house where the keys were hung up and surrendered before an electronic gate opened to that of freedom & with this in mind Sue began to drill Veronica of all details relating to this calculated but daring escape bid, also David would be contacted on the second mobile as Sue realised that a high volume of calls that would be irregular leading up to the escape would throw suspicion in that of her direction, David would assist in helping Veronica with transportation with of course a third party collecting her from the main car park outside of Gladstonville, a third party would also purchase the air fare to freedom in that of the name of Maria Stanovich direct from the airport with cash as no record of any bank card transaction could relate David in his assistance to Sue & her lover, so with David doing his bit, Sue would also concentrate on her part in the escape plot, again & again Sue would drum into Veronica the very last details of her last steps to freedom but would look also at the perfect "window of opportunity" to give the desired time scale for success of Veronica's freedom which would be after careful reflection during just after a shift change as there would normally be very little activity in the main gate house usually 10 to fifteen minutes after a main shift change & so on the basis of this the game plan was put clearly in place & a time and date now apparent, both lovers continued their plans with full vigour, one week before the escape Veronica had received an anonymous letter which had been sent to her by Brian Lawson who had mixed feelings as to whether he had been placed in anything untoward and underhanded as Ricky had been murdered and also Mary within days of the photographs of Ricky's infidelity with Franchesca being handed to Jay Edwards, and so without incriminating himself with his anonymity he stated that Jay Edwards who she knew had been behind the photographs, Veronica shocked to say the least was feeling confused to say the least, but also knew Jay was bitter with regards to everything that his cunning & devious wife had done to him & so she started to build a picture that Jay was behind a revenge plot with regards to the photographs and was now boiling with rage to say the least and so she would suspend her feelings but would now use this as the catalyst in her bid for freedom, and so with her inner feelings now on hold, her dedication and onus would be placed on the escape plan & so with Sue Haymen and brother David a time & date would be set, David would be given the exact time & date that the escape would take place & from this a neighbouring airport would be checked for flights directly out of the U/K, unfortunately a direct flight within the window of opportunity directly out of British jurisdiction direct to Cyprus was not available, however David had done his homework & therefore on reflection a direct flight for check in etc within the window of opportunity direct to Istanbul in Turkey was feasible & therefore even if Maria Stanovich was identified as Veronica Lapland after the subsequent inquiry David would with his underworld connections have Veronica brought over to Northern Cyprus by boat & a secondary identity given to Veronica with an entry stamp finalised by a corrupt Customs official. David had left nothing to chance and with his side of the bargain all the emphasis would now rest with the two lovers & as planned Sue was prepared for the biggest gamble of her life one of which she was now ready to gamble & so the time had arrived and Sue assisted with all the pre planning to dress Veronica with the 1960 style black bob wig and similar make up from that of her make up bag discussing over & over again the last details of the escape plot as she applied the make up to her lover & before tying Governor Haymen up, Sue explained the last details, "take this mobile with you & if you make it outside the main gate it will ring", "walk 500 metres directly straight in front of you", "you will then be assisted, to where you will be given your new identity & taken to the airport", "ask no questions, just follow the instructions given to you", "O.K.", replied Veronica with every last detail discussed & finalised Veronica now dressed in Sue's clothing took her keys & chain with one question, "darling how will I know which keys are which", "don't worry my love", replied a stripped Sue, "my earliest childhood memory was of my father bouncing me on his knee with the nursery rhyme from the colours of the rainbow", "you know, red & yellow & pink & green", "and therefore think the colours of the rainbow of which I have identified the keys with". "Here are the keys to your freedom", the first door out of this wing, there is a small red mark, the second has a yellow mark, the third & final key to your freedom is pink, remember after opening each of the doors to scrape the small colour coded paint for these keys off with your nails Veronica after each exit", O.K. replied Veronica, "now come on Veronica we haven't much time", with the keys in hand & donning the distinctive appearance of that of Governor Haymen, Veronica as pre planned began to tie & gag her lover up & when complete Sue insisted that before the gag was placed around her mouth she should assault her to make the hostage scene "realistic", Veronica was reluctant to hurt her lover but Sue was looking at the bigger picture & with this took hold of Veronica's hand and scraped it fiercely down that of her own face, blood now apparent on Sue's face & the final gag placed around her mouth, Veronica now determined to make good of that of her escape proceeded to the main hall & walked directly to the reception area her heart pulsating and bursting at the seams she placed the yellow coded key into the main gate to the courtyard, her heart beating faster she was unchallenged as she now walked into the fresh air & proceeded to the gate house, she was now feeling more & more nervous as she approached the main gate house scraping with her nail as her lover had told her to do so, the first of the colour codes, the last hurdle & finishing line in site, she paused for one last gasp of air & opened the main door for the gate house to hang the keys up & surrendered them, with this as her heart beat fiercely more so, she turned and walked towards the main electronic gate for it to electronically open, a voice shouted in the distance "Goodnight Ma'am", she paused, but quickly answered back "Goodnight", she stood all but sheepishly waiting for the tap on the shoulder thinking she had been uncovered, but to her astonishment the electronic gate opened, she had thought of the colours of the rainbow & now all dark clouds that hung over her had disappeared as she could see her rainbow, she walked as planned the 500 metres and the mobile given to her by Veronica rang, she placed it to her ear and within seconds a car pulled up alongside her with "Veronica", yes replied Veronica, "get in quick we haven't much time, she was handed her new E.U. passport and other documentation, she could not believe how elaborate her passport picture of herself & the new cloned identity of that of Maria Stanovich had been so well hand crafted, without asking any questions her guide handed her the flight tickets to her new life. With a simple "good luck & remain calm, just look the officials straight in the eye, & don't panic", Veronica now proceeded to the main entrance of the airport with one piece of unfinished business on her mind, that being Jay Edwards, the anonymous letter she had received had that of Jay Edwards mobile number on it, she had not said anything to Sue, but had kept the number and made a phone call to that number. An unexpecting Jay Edwards answered the phone, "Hello", Veronica quickly answered, "it's Veronica Lapland", "surprise, surprise Jay", "just to let you know that now I am on to you remember to always look over your shoulder wherever you may be", "because now it's my turn", Veronica immediately switched the telephone off and proceeded to Departures, Jay shell shocked looked very concerned to say the least as far from being "untouchable", he too was now the intended target, Veronica going through Customs did everything she was asked of and successfully boarded Flight MK 4716 to Istanbul now airborne, Sue back at Gladstonville was just about to be uncovered, she too had played a great part in this, she had for the last 10 minutes, before Veronica was airborne been rolling around on the office floor fiercely to make her hostage plight that all the more realistic, now discovered & untied she screamed out "Lapland has taken my keys quick as you can", with Gladstonville now completely locked down, the escape established with a lot of red faces, Sue Haymen started to shout & scream to all of her staff to inform the Home Office & also the Police that prisoner Lapland had escaped & was charged with two counts of murder & was extremely dangerous, with this all ports & airports were sealed, however the escape was perfectly executed & therefore the arrival of Detective Inspector Lee Knott & his partner Detective Sergeant Jim Carey was a fruitless exercise except to follow protocol of the details of her hostage ordeal & assault, tired & drained after her interview, Governor Haymen returned home that evening & returned to work the following day to be greeted by Home Office Minister for Prisons Miss Caroline Jones, a no nonsense graduate who did not suffer fools & did not take any prisoners & with a high profile murderer escaping & being given such a trusted position whilst awaiting sentence, Miss Jones was straight to the point with, "I understand the Police have taken a statement from you Haymen", "yes Ma'am", "this is very embarrassing for us & given the fact that you placed such a high profile prisoner in such a position of trust leaves serious question marks over your judgement therefore I have no alternative but to suspend you pending a full internal enquiry", "but Mamm", "there are no buts Haymen clear your desk, your replacement arrives in just under one hour". "Just one thing more Haymen, your badge please", with Sue now suspended a shocked Jay Edwards had watched the news unfolding especially with the phone call the previous evening with a new sense of panic as he now realised he too could become part of Veronica's deadly games.

THE END

ISBN 142515833-1
9 781425 158330

Printed in Great Britain
by Amazon.co.uk, Ltd.,
Marston Gate.